Aldrin thought he knew
**everything.**

He knew how to put up a tent . . .

. . . eventually.

He knew how to identify plants.
'This is the leaf of a tree.'

He knew how to tie fancy knots.
'A tangle-wangle knot!'

How to read animal tracks.

'Raccoon footprints.'

And how to make tools with sticks.
'A tail support!'

Fox, Rabbit, and Woodpecker
looked on with
amazement.

But Hubble and Lovell were more interested in looking up at the night sky.

'There's the Great Bear!'

'And the Little Bear!'

'Silly bears!' said Aldrin. 'Everyone knows
there are no animals in the sky. Just lots
of stars and a big round moon.'

One night Aldrin invited everyone to toast marshmallows over his campfire.

Rabbit had a question. 'Aldrin,' she asked, 'why isn't the moon so round tonight?'

Hubble and Lovell thought they knew but Aldrin wasn't going to ask them. It would show that he had no idea.

Instead he just tried to sound important and said, 'I think we need a proper investigation. Come to my tent tomorrow night.'

The next day, on her way to Aldrin's, Rabbit
spotted Hubble and Lovell going the other way.
They were wearing funny helmets.

And when she reached Aldrin's tent, Hubble and Lovell were not there. Rabbit told Aldrin, Woodpecker, and Fox about the funny helmets.

'I know what those are,' said Aldrin, 'they're space helmets. I wonder what those bears are up to?'

Later that week, Fox bumped into Hubble and
Lovell carrying a long, heavy parcel.

To be collected
by Hubble
and Lovell

'What have you got there?' he asked.

'Sorry, too busy to stop
and chat,' they replied.

Fox ran all the way
to Moon Rescue HQ
to report . . .

. . . the long parcel incident.

'I know what that is,' said Aldrin, 'it's a space rocket. I think those bears have got something to do with the disappearing moon.'

Woodpecker volunteered to watch the bears more closely.

And over the next few days she spotted . . .

Hubble and Lovell . . .

Several times.

She even saw them driving a truck full of rubble!

Hubble and Lovell

Woodpecker staggered back to Moon Rescue HQ with a piece of rubble as evidence.

'I know what that is,' said Aldrin, 'it's moon rock! Hubble and Lovell have been stealing the moon.'

Over the next few nights, everyone became
very busy at Moon Rescue HQ. But there
was hardly any moon left to rescue.

Just then Hubble and Lovell arrived.
'Evening all,' they said.

'Would you like to come to our new den
and see the moon?' said Hubble.

'I knew it,
I knew it!'
said Aldrin.
'You **have** been
stealing the moon.'

Lovell just continued calmly.
'You'll be able to see how rocky it is . . .

# . . . with our new telescope!

'Oh,' said Aldrin, feeling a bit ashamed.
'It looks like I was wrong. I'm sorry
for being such a silly know-it-all.'

'Don't worry!' laughed Hubble and
Lovell. 'Step inside!'

The bears certainly knew **a lot**
about the moon . . .

HUbble and Lovell
**MOON
EXPERIENCE**
→

. . . they knew how long it takes the moon to go around the earth.

**27 days, 7 hours, 43 minutes, and 11.6 seconds!**

They knew what to call the moon when it is getting smaller . . .

**Waning!**

until it can't be seen at all.

**A NEW moon!**

And they knew what to call the moon when it is getting bigger . . .

**Waxing!**

until all of it can be seen.

**A FULL moon!**

Everyone was amazed.

But Rabbit had a new question. 'How many stars are there in the sky?' she asked.

Hubble and Lovell had no idea.

'I know, I know!' Squealed Aldrin.

'Do you really?' sighed the others. 'Yes!' said Aldrin. 'There are . . .

...far too many

For our friends Julie, Alan, Sean, and Jude xxxx

And in memory of some great space explorers
who left this world while I was creating this book:
Neil Armstrong, Sir Bernard Lovell, and Sir Patrick Moore.

# OXFORD
## UNIVERSITY PRESS

Great Clarendon Street, Oxford OX2 6DP

Oxford University Press is a department of the University of Oxford.
It furthers the University's objective of excellence in research,
scholarship, and education by publishing worldwide in

Oxford  New York

Auckland  Cape Town  Dar es Salaam  Hong Kong  Karachi
Kuala Lumpur  Madrid  Melbourne  Mexico City  Nairobi
New Delhi  Shanghai  Taipei  Toronto

With offices in
Argentina  Austria  Brazil  Chile  Czech Republic  France  Greece
Guatemala  Hungary  Italy  Japan  Poland  Portugal  Singapore
South Korea  Switzerland  Thailand  Turkey  Ukraine  Vietnam

Oxford is a registered trade mark of Oxford University Press
in the UK and in certain other countries

Text and illustrations © Richard Byrne 2014

The moral rights of the author/illustrator have been asserted
Database right Oxford University Press (maker)

First published in 2014

British Library Cataloguing in Publication Data
Data available

ISBN: 978-0-19-273503-4 (hardback)
ISBN: 978-0-19-273504-1 (paperback)

10 9 8 7 6 5 4 3 2 1

Printed in China

Paper used in the production of this book is a natural,
recyclable product made from wood grown in sustainable forests.
The manufacturing process conforms to the environmental
regulations of the country of origin.